Donna Magazine Movies

Donna Magazine Movies

By

Donna KAKONGE

ISBN: 9798353097440

Printed in the United States

Cover Design

By

Donna KAKONGE

Table of Contents

The Scary Night

The Scary Night

It was a dark and stormy night. Phillip had been driving home from work, and was now about an hour away from his house. He had made it the last few miles, but was now in the throes of a full-blown panic attack. His breaths came in short gasps and his heart was pounding so hard, it felt like it was trying to escape his chest. He pulled to the side of the road, scattering gravel, and tried to calm himself. He closed his eyes and took several deep breaths before starting the car. He crept along the road, his car the only light in a wide and dark world. The rain continued to beat against the windshield like tiny fists.

Suddenly, Phillip saw something moving in the ditch beside him and he screamed, slamming on the brakes. Nothing appeared there in the darkness but he could still see movement out of the corner of his eye. He started to drive again but only made it a few feet before slamming on the brakes once more as something ran into the road in front of him. This time, there was no mistake - it was a person, staggering towards him blindly through the downpour.

Phillip's heart raced even faster as he realized that he was being targeted. Who could be doing this? Why were they doing this? He tried to back up but there was another figure standing just behind his car, blocking his way out. Terror washed over him as he sat paralyzed behind the wheel. The figures began to converge on his car and Phillip knew that he wasn't going to make it out alive...

She looked over the edge of the building, her heart racing as she contemplated jumping. She had been through so much pain and suffering in her life, and she just couldn't take it anymore. She was tired of being beaten down, tired of being a victim.

But as she took another step closer to the edge, she heard

someone calling out to her. It was a voice she recognized, a voice that had once given her hope. She turned around to see who was calling to her, and saw him running towards her.

He reached her just in time to pull her back from the edge, and they collapsed together on the ground. He hugged her tightly as she cried tears of relief and happiness. They had been through so much together, but they had finally made it through.

You're driving home from work, and you can't wait to get there. You've had a long day, and all you want is to relax in your own bed. As you turn the corner, you see the house...but something's not right. The lights are on, but there's no car in the driveway. You pull into the garage and notice that the door is open. You park your car and get out, but as soon as you step out of the garage, someone grabs you from behind!

The Detective

The Detective

In a world of ever-growing technology, some things never change. Detective John Mojo is back on the job, and he's ready to solve another murder. As he starts investigating the victim's life, he begins to realize that this case is more complicated than he thought. With suspects abound and no clear lead, Mojo will have to use all of his skills to catch the killer before it's too late.

The sun had just set, and the sky was ablaze with colors. The cool autumn breeze rustled the leaves of the trees, and a light mist began to form over the ground. All was still in the forest, except for one creature that moved through the underbrush. It was a deer, and it was running for its life.

Suddenly, out of nowhere, a pack of wolves appeared, chasing after the poor deer. The deer ran as fast as it could, but the wolves were faster. They soon caught up to their prey and attacked. The deer fought back bravely, but there were too many wolves. In the end, they overpowered it and killed it.

The alpha wolf stood over the dead deer, victorious. He proudly displayed his kill to his packmates, who howled in approval. Then they began to feast on the carcass, ripping into it with their sharp teeth.

When Madison moves to the small town of Mojang, she

doesn't expect to find love. But after meeting the handsome and mysterious Max, she can't help but be drawn in by his charm.

As they get to know each other better, Madison realizes that there's more to Max than meets the eye. He seems like he's hiding something, and she can't help but feel like he's in danger.

Can Madison figure out what's going on before it's too late? And will she finally find love in Mojang?

The Hunters

The Hunters

Jane and Gerald were fighting for their lives. They had been lost in the rainforest for days, and they were running out of time. They needed to find a way to save the rainforest before it was too late.

But they weren't alone in the forest. There were dangerous hunters who wanted to kill them, and they were doing everything they could to stay alive.

The hunters were relentless, and Jane and Gerald were constantly on the run. But they refused to give up. They knew that if they didn't save the rainforest, it would be lost forever.

Jane and Gerald had been hiking through the rainforest for hours, trying to save it from the hunters. They had been warned about the hunters before they set out, but they didn't think it would be this dangerous. The hunters were after them, and they were running for their lives. "We have to keep going," Gerald said, panting for breath. "If we can make it to the other side of the forest, we'll be safe." Jane nodded, even though she didn't really believe it. They had been running for what felt like hours, and they were getting tired. Then they heard the sound of twigs snapping behind them. The hunters were close. "Hurry!" Gerald exclaimed, pushing Jane in front of him as they ran faster. They could hear the hunters closing in on them, and they knew that they wouldn't make it to safety. Suddenly, there was a loud gunshot and Gerald fell to the ground. Jane turned around and saw that he was dead. She couldn't believe it – her best friend was gone because of these ruthless hunters. The hunters came closer, and Jane knew that she was next. But then something miraculous happened – a group of animals came out of nowhere and attacked the hunters! They were finally saved!

Jane and Gerald had been in the rainforest for days, fighting for their survival. They were trying to save the rainforest from being destroyed, but they were constantly running into dangerous hunters who wanted to kill them.

The hunters were relentless in their pursuit of Jane and Gerald, and they seemed to be getting closer and closer every day. Finally, after weeks of dodging bullets and avoiding traps, Jane and Gerald found themselves cornered by the hunters.

There was no escape – they would have to fight or die. In a desperate attempt to save themselves, Jane and Gerald fought with all their might, but, unfortunately, they were outnumbered and outmatched. The hunters brutally killed them both...

The Squirrels

The Squirrels

The squirrels were the best of friends.
Every day, they would spend hours playing together in the forest.
The humans nearby would watch them, fascinated by their antics.
One day, the humans got lost in the forest.
They tried to use the same methods as the squirrels to find their way back home.
But it was no use.
They were hopelessly lost.

Suddenly, they heard a voice coming from nearby.
It was one of the squirrels!
The squirrel had found them and was leading them back home.
The humans were so grateful to the squirrel for saving them.
They thanked him over and over again.
The squirrel just looked at them with his big, brown eyes and blinked happily.
The squirrels were friends.
Every day, the two humans would spend hours watching

them play and chatter away to each other.
They were fascinated by how the squirrels used their body language to communicate, and soon started doing the same thing themselves whenever they got lost in the forest.
One day, they decided to follow the squirrels a little further than usual.
Suddenly, they heard rustling in the bushes and saw a deer staring at them with its big brown eyes.

The deer didn't move, so the humans slowly backed away until they were safe again.
They turned to look at the squirrels, who were perched high up in a tree watching them intently.
The humans smiled and waved goodbye before following the squirrels back home.
The four friends were walking through the forest, trying to find their way back to the campsite.
It was getting dark and they were starting to get lost.

Suddenly, the two squirrels appeared.

The friends were amazed at how the squirrels could talk with their bodies.

They started copying the squirrels, giving themselves directions in the forest.

It wasn't long before they found their way back to the campsite.

The friends thanked the squirrels for their help and said goodbye.

About the Author

Multiple award-winning author/teacher/journalist/online lawyer/retired college professor/videographer/podcaster with over **30** years of writing expertise. Produced **15** daily articles for the *Toronto Star* and Young People's Press. **Six** stories hourly for the Canadian Broadcasting Corporation (CBC) for the radio and television news. There are three current daily affairs radio stories **5** days a week in English and French for Radio

Canada International (RCI). Owner of Donna Magazine since October 1, 2007. The magazine has more than **10,900** multi-media articles and an audience of more than a billion people. The magazine is based on paid Donna Magazine Membership Inclusion. More than **42** years of experience teaching multi-platform writing at the college level worldwide, plus journalism, legal, and communications experience. Author, editor, the ghostwriter of more than **290** books, mainly self-published. Expertise in audio and video editing with industry-standard software. Expert editor with Grammarly Premium possession. With **155,215** books sold so far—six books in the Toronto Public Library and **29** other libraries throughout North America. With **92** of her titles in the online library, BIBLIOBOARD connected with the Toronto Public Library. Highest level of education a doctorate from the best university in Canada. Expert knowledge of both British and

American written and spoken English. Undergraduate journalism degree, master's media studies degree, and doctorate education degree from the best schools in Canada. Law degree from a school in London, England. Teaching English as a Second Language certificate from an American school. Digital Humanities certificate from the non-profit unit of Harvard University, best American school. Dr. Donna Kay Cindy KAKONGE, BJ (Carleton University - Ottawa), MA (Concordia University -

Montréal), TESOL (LINGUAEDGE - Online, United States), LLB (University of London International PROGRAMMES), EdD (OISE | University of Toronto)

www.ingramcontent.com/pod-product-compliance
Lightning Source LLC
LaVergne TN
LVHW091243150826
845673LV00003B/1269

* 9 7 9 8 3 5 3 0 9 7 4 4 0 *